Nature Sticker Stories

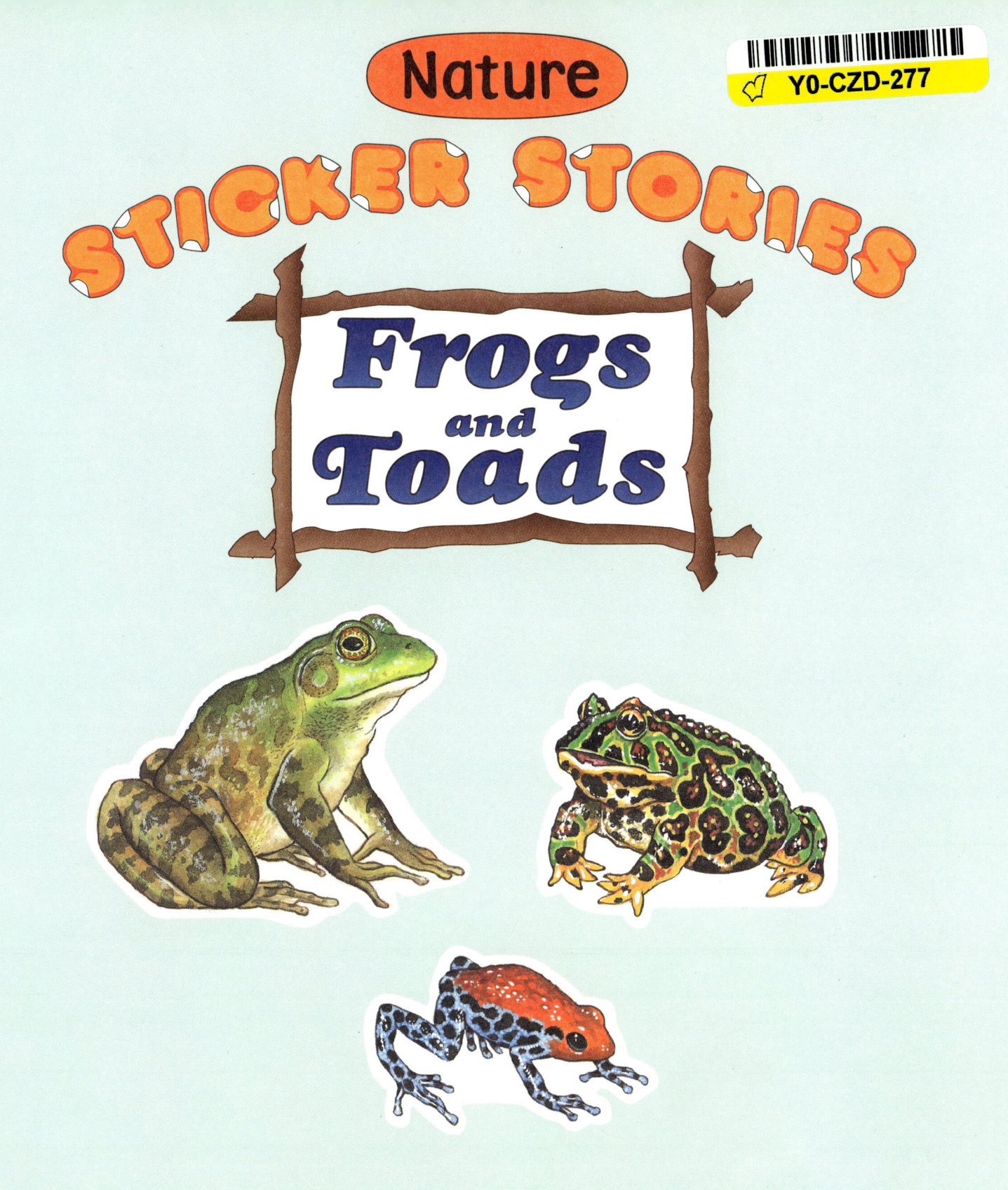

Frogs and Toads

Illustrated by Katy Bratun

GROSSET & DUNLAP • NEW YORK

Copyright © 1998 by Grosset & Dunlap, Inc. Illustrations copyright © 1998 by Katy Bratun. All rights reserved. Published by Grosset & Dunlap, Inc., a member of Penguin Putnam Books for Young Readers, New York. GROSSET & DUNLAP is a trademark of Grosset & Dunlap, Inc. Published simultaneously in Canada. Printed in Singapore.
ISBN 0-448-41859-2   A B C D E F G H I J

Frogs and toads are amphibians. Amphibians can live on land and in water.

Some frogs and toads live in the desert.
They don't need a lot of water.

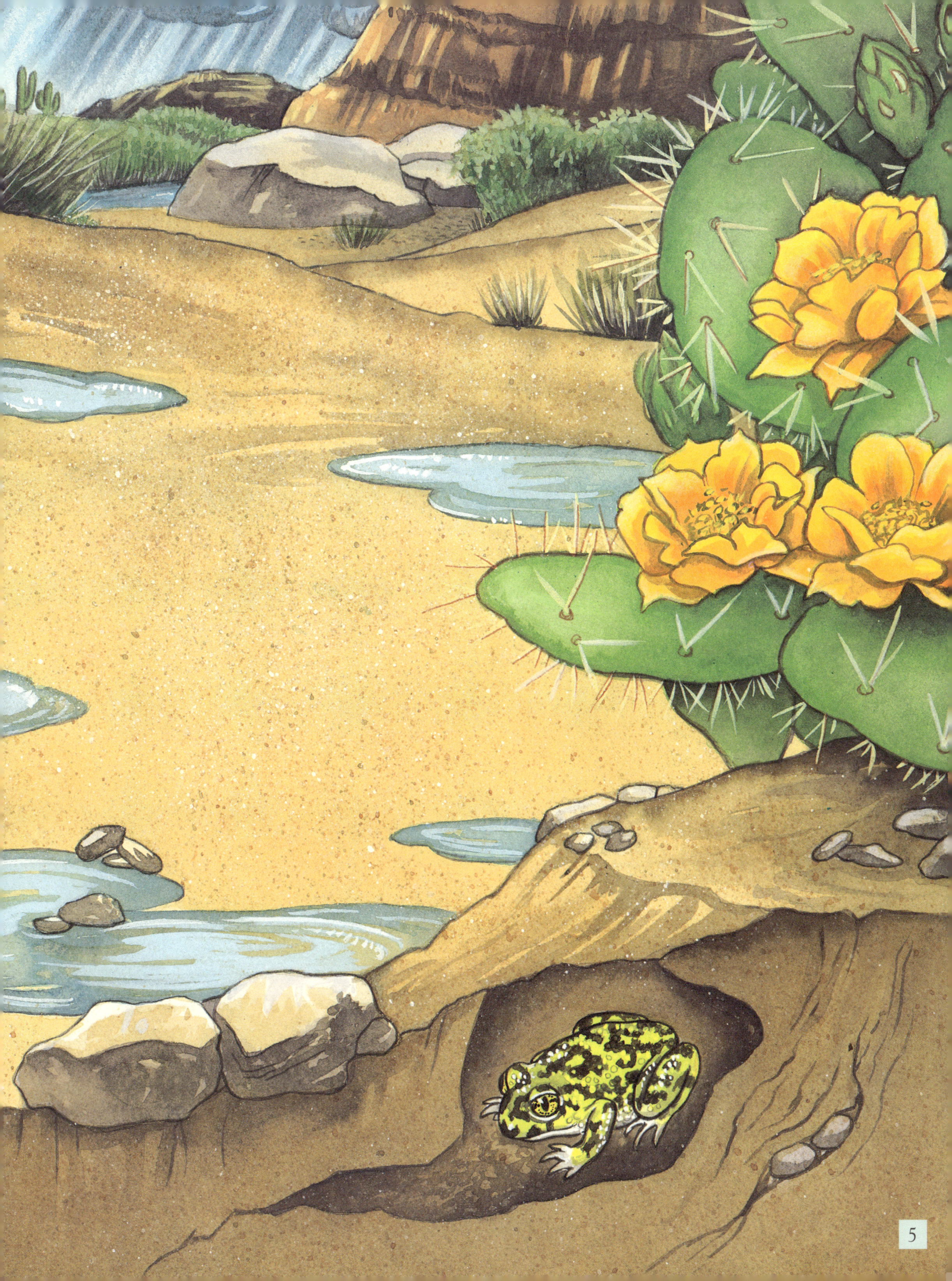

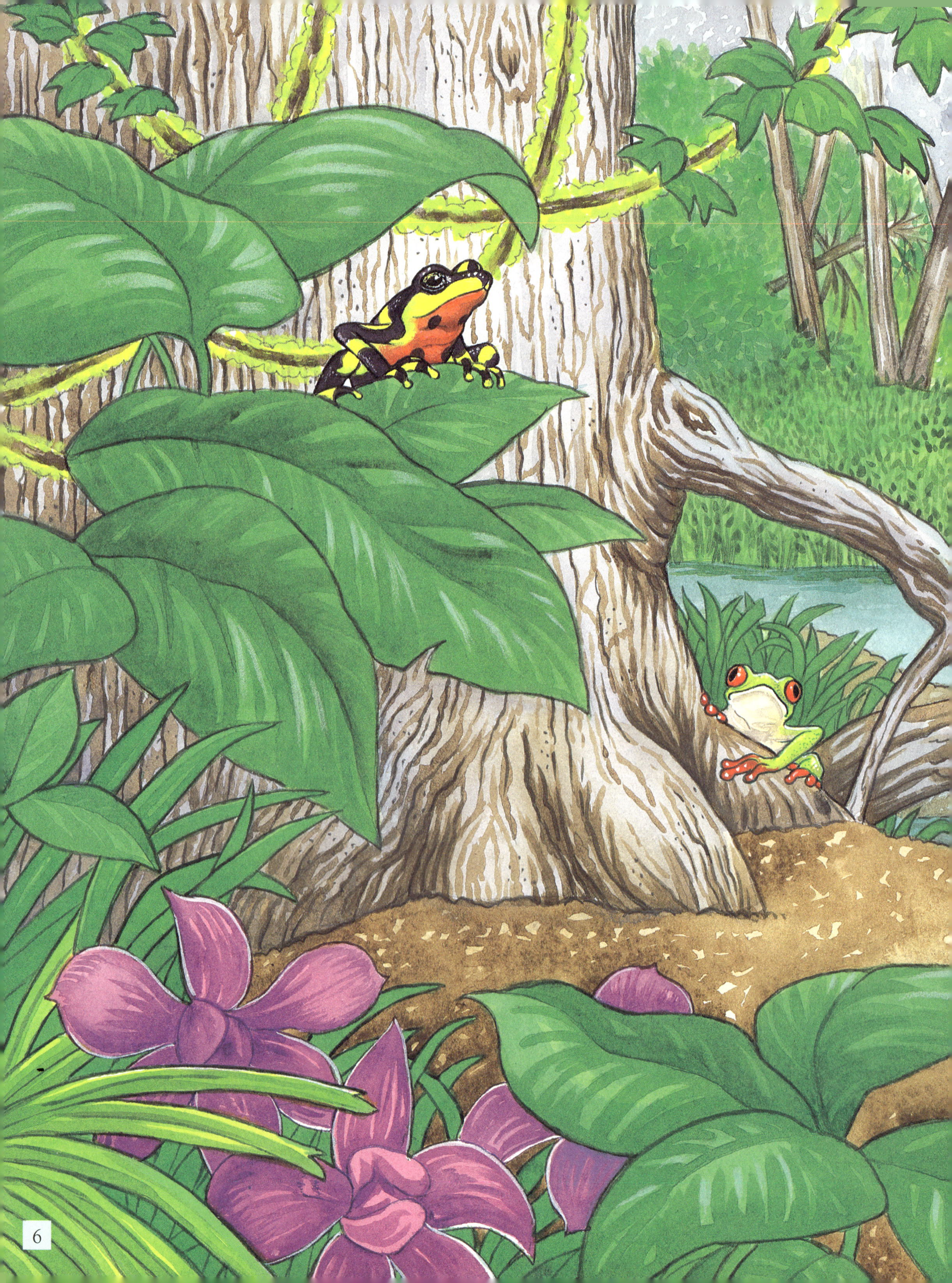

Baby frogs and toads look like little fish. They are called tadpoles. When they get older, they lose their tails and grow legs.

BULLFROG TADPOLE

BULLFROG

AMERICAN TOAD

AMERICAN TOAD

COMMON GRAY TREEFROG

In the evening, frogs and toads puff out their throats and make noises. This is their way of calling to each other.

13

These frogs are pretty with their bright colors.
But their skin is very poisonous.
Other animals know to stay away!

Frogs and toads are helpful, too.
They eat lots of pesky bugs!